I am an ARO PUBLISHING THIRTY WORD BOOK
My thirty words are:

a	how	sea
be	I	sent
call (called)	if	spaceman
cowboy	in	that
Daddy	it's (it) (is)	the
diver	maybe	twice
Doctor	me	when
for	nice	will
from	phone	would
get	President	Vet

ISBN 0-89868-189-8 — Library Bound
ISBM 0-89868-190-1 — Soft Bound

My First
Phonecall

Story by Julia Allen
Pictures by Bob Reese

ARO PUBLISHING

A phone call.

A phone call for Daddy.

A phone call for me.

When will that be?

It would be nice

if a spaceman called twice.

How would it be

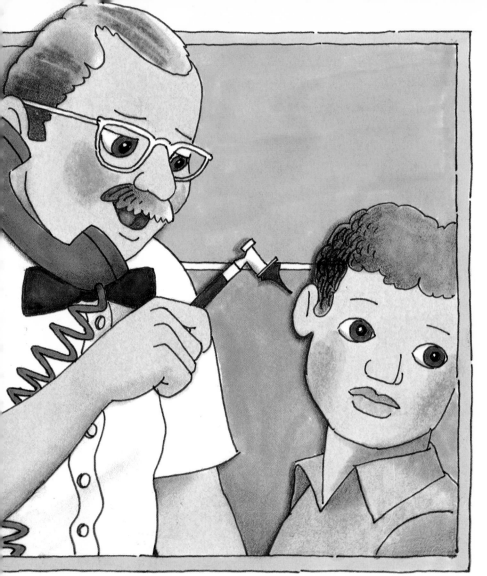

if a Doctor called me?

Maybe I will get

a phone call from the Vet.

A phone call for me

from a diver in the sea?

How would it be

if a cowboy called me?

A phone call is sent

from the President!

A phone call for me?

It's from Daddy!